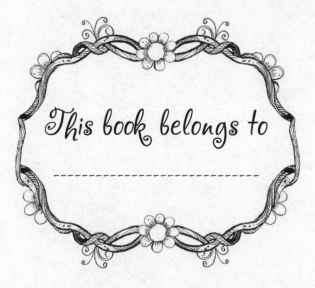

This book belongs to

Bluebell Glade

Dandelion Dell

Heart of Misty Wood

Hawthorn Hedgerows

How many **Fairy Animals** books have you collected?

- 🌼 Chloe the Kitten
- 🌼 Bella the Bunny
- 🌼 Paddy the Puppy
- ✅ Mia the Mouse

And there are more magical adventures coming very soon!

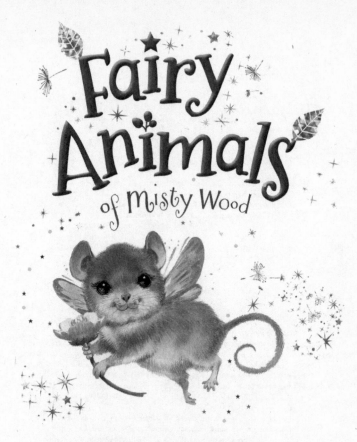

Fairy Animals
of Misty Wood

Mia the Mouse

Lily Small

Henry Holt and Company
New York

With special thanks to Thea Bennett

Henry Holt and Company, LLC
Publishers since 1866
175 Fifth Avenue
New York, New York 10010
mackids.com

First published in the United States in 2015 by Henry Holt and Company, LLC.
Originally published in Great Britain in 2013
by Egmont UK Limited.

Library of Congress Cataloging-in-Publication Data
Small, Lily.
Mia the mouse / Lily Small. — First American edition.
pages cm. — (Fairy animals of Misty Wood ; 4)
"Originally published in Great Britain in 2013 by Egmont UK Limited."
Summary: Mia is in the middle of telling a story to her sick grandmother when her mother
asks her to run an errand, but, distracted by what may come next in the story, all Mia can
remember is that she is to fetch something that starts with "B." Includes activities.
ISBN 978-1-62779-144-1 (paperback) — ISBN 978-1-62779-363-6 (e-book)
[1. Fairies—Fiction. 2. Mice—Fiction. 3. Storytelling—Fiction. 4. Bees—Fiction.] I. Title.
PZ7.S6385Mi 2015   [Fic]—dc23   2014047285

Henry Holt books may be purchased for business or promotional use.
For information on bulk purchases, please contact the Macmillan Corporate
and Premium Sales Department at (800) 221-7945 x5442 or by e-mail
at specialmarkets@macmillan.com.

First American Edition—2015
Printed in the United States of America by R. R. Donnelley &
Sons Company, Harrisonburg, Virginia

1 3 5 7 9 10 8 6 4 2

Contents

CHAPTER ONE

A Good Little Mouse

Deep in the Heart of Misty Wood, there was an oak tree so tall its branches seemed to touch the sky. Its leaves were as green as

emeralds, and they loved to dance
in the breeze. The oak tree's thick,
knobby roots stretched deep into
the soil and held the tree steady.

If you looked carefully, in
between the tree roots, behind
a cluster of tall green ferns, you
would see a hole leading down to
a cozy burrow. And if you looked
very carefully indeed, you would
see a little mouse sitting on the
grass next to the hole. The mouse's

2

name was Mia, and she lived in
the burrow with her mom and dad,
her grandma, and her four baby
brothers and sisters.

Mia was a Moss Mouse—one
of the fairy animals of Misty Wood.
Her beautiful fairy wings were

transparent, just like a dragonfly's, and when the sunshine touched them, they twinkled violet and green. Her fur was as golden as honey— except on her tummy, where it was snow white—and she had long, silky whiskers that wiggled and twirled whenever she was excited.

Mia was making a cushion from a ball of soft green moss.

"Pat-a-cake, pat-a-cake, pat-a-cake!" she sang to herself as she

rolled the moss along the ground and patted it into a nice round shape with her tiny pink paws.

Just like all the fairy animals of Misty Wood, the Moss Mice had a special job to do to make the wood a wonderful place to live. The mice made soft, squishy cushions out of moss and placed them all around the wood so the other fairy animals would have somewhere comfortable to sit.

"Pat, pat, pat!" Mia sang as she shaped the cushion.

"Hello, Mia!" a voice called.

There was a scrabbling noise from inside the hole, and a face with bright beady eyes and long silvery whiskers popped out. It was Mia's dad.

"I'm afraid Grandma's come down with a nasty case of the sniffles," he said. "Will you go and keep her company? Mom's busy

7

with the babies, and I've got to go out and collect some more moss for our cushions."

"Of course I will," Mia said.

Mia's dad gave her a twinkly-eyed smile. "You *are* a good little mouse! Perhaps you could tell Grandma one of your stories. I bet she would appreciate it." And with that, he jumped out of the hole, twirled his whiskers, and unfurled his wings. They glinted silver in

the sun. "See you at teatime!" Mia's dad called as he flew off through the trees. He carried a big bag made from spider silk in his front paws.

Mia picked up her cushion and hurried underground. The passageway to the burrow was nice and cool and smelled of fresh earth. Mia's whiskers began to twitch. Telling stories was her favorite thing in the whole wide world. She loved it even more than making cushions.

Mia scampered into the burrow. At one end, her mom was busy feeding the babies. At the other, Grandma was tucked into her bed of soft moss.

Mia hopped over to her. Grandma was curled up in the middle of the bed with her nose peeping over the edge. Normally, Grandma's nose was pale pink, but today it was red. Mia got a little closer. Normally, Grandma's black

eyes shone and there was a happy smile on her face, but today her eyes were bleary and she looked sad.

"A-a-a-a-CHOO!" Grandma sneezed when she saw Mia.

"Bless you!" said Mia. She hopped onto the cushion she'd just made and leaned her front paws on the edge of the bed. "Dad said you weren't feeling well, so I've come to keep you company."

"Ah, thank you, Mia," replied Grandma, wiping her nose on a white daisy petal. Then she sneezed again. "A-a-a-CHOO!"

"Oh, dear. You must be feeling awful," Mia said.

12

"Yes, I am." Grandma sighed.

"My poor nose is so sore . . .

a-a-a-CHOO!"

Mia tilted her head to one side.

"Would you like me to tell you a story?"

Grandma's eyes lit up. "Ooh, yes, please! I do love your stor— a-a-a-CHOO!"

Mia sat back on her cushion. If she could think of a really good story, Grandma might forget about her sneezes and her sore nose.

Mia's whiskers wiggled with excitement as a story began to form in her mind: "Once upon a

time . . . there was a caterpillar!"
she started.

"A caterpillar? Well, I never,"
said Grandma with a loud sniff.

"And she was named
Clarissa!" said Mia.

"That's a big name for a little
caterpillar," said Grandma.

"Oh, but she wasn't little!"
cried Mia, and her whiskers
twitched and wiggled so much
she had to jump down and run

15

around Grandma's bed. "She was the biggest caterpillar you've ever seen! She was bigger than you and me and Mom and Dad and all the babies put together!"

"Goodness," said Grandma. Then she smiled. She hadn't sneezed for quite a while now. "How did she get to be so big?"

"Well . . . ," began Mia, jumping back onto the cushion, "Clarissa was very

16

greedy. She ate and ate and ate, all

day long."

Grandma frowned. "Wherever did she get all that food from?"

Mia's whiskers quivered as she thought up the answer. "Clarissa had a best friend. His name was Archie, and he was a tiny ant. Archie brought Clarissa lots of snacks. He brought her leaves and berries and nuts and—"

"Lucky Clarissa!" said Grandma, wriggling upright. She looked much happier now.

Mia sat up on her hind legs as the next part of the story came into her head. "But one day—and this is the really scary bit of the story, Grandma—Clarissa disappeared!"

"Oh, dear!" said Grandma. "Where had she gone?"

Mia sighed. "Nobody knew. Archie searched all through Misty Wood, but he couldn't find her anywhere."

19

Grandma shook her head, and her whiskers began to droop. "That's a very sad story."

Mia was about to explain that she hadn't finished yet when her mom came scampering over to them.

"Thank you for looking after Grandma, Mia," she said. "The babies are asleep now, so I'll take over from you."

Mia sighed. She was just

20

getting to the most exciting part of the story.

"It's all right, Mom, *I'm* looking after Grandma," she said.

Mia's mom smiled. Then she stroked the moss cushion that Mia had just made. "What a lovely soft cushion. Well done, Mia. There's just one thing—"

"Oh, Mom, I'm in the middle of telling Grandma a story!" Mia interrupted.

"I know," Mia's mom said. "But I just need you to fetch something for me."

Mia sighed. She wanted to go on with her story. She wanted to give it the best, most exciting ending ever so that Grandma would forget all about being sick.

"It's all right, Mia," Grandma said. "I'm feeling a bit tired, so I'll have a nap and you can tell me the rest later. I'll look forward to that."

22

Grandma yawned and curled up in her lovely warm bed, ready to fall fast asleep.

Mia thought about where Clarissa the caterpillar could have disappeared to, so she could tell her grandma later.

"I need you to bring me some bluebells," Mia's mom said. "You can do that, can't you, Mia?"

"Easy-peasy," said Mia.

But she was still thinking about

the story. *Where, oh, where would Archie find Clarissa?*

Mia's mom looked at her. "Are you sure you won't forget? I know what you're like when you're making up one of your stories— you never have room in your head to think about anything else! Try to remember: I need you to get me some bluebells."

"Yes, yes, bluebells, I know, Mom," Mia said as she hopped

24

down from the cushion. *Maybe Clarissa could be hiding in a big, spooky cave? Maybe she got caught in a giant cobweb?*

"Sleep well, Grandma," Mia called as she scampered through the burrow. *Maybe Clarissa got stuck inside a rabbit hole?*

Mia raced through the tunnel that led into Misty Wood. She jumped out of the little hole between the roots, opened her

25

gauzy wings, and floated up, up, up into the sunshine.

"Clarissa the Giant Caterpillar! My best story ever!" the little Moss Mouse squeaked happily as she fluttered away.

CHAPTER TWO

Don't Forget . . .

Mia's wings glimmered and shone
as she flew through the bright
sunlight.

"I can't forget," she muttered

to herself. "Mom wants me to bring her some . . . ooh! What's that?"

Bright green leaves were hanging down from an oak tree nearby. They had huge holes in them, as if something had been eating them.

"Maybe a giant caterpillar ate those leaves!" Mia gasped. Her whiskers were twitching like mad. "Maybe it was Clarissa!"

She swooped down to take a closer look.

The leaves did look just like Clarissa had been chomping them with her greedy munching jaws.

Mia landed on the tree branch and skipped along it. Maybe she would find a real-life Clarissa up

here! She searched everywhere, peering under the leaves, but she couldn't see a giant caterpillar.

I'm just like Archie the Ant! Mia thought with a smile. *I'm hunting for Clarissa!*

Mia leaped off the branch and flitted between the trees. She had to get home to the burrow right away to tell Grandma the next part of her story. But . . . wait a minute!

The little Moss Mouse came

30

to a halt. Her mom had asked her to get something. What was it? She thought and thought, but she couldn't remember. Her head was too full of thoughts about Clarissa and Archie.

"Think, Mia, think!" she squeaked.

I need you to bring me some b . . .

It was no good. Next, she tried saying it out loud: "I need you to bring me some b . . ." But, try as

31

she might, she couldn't remember what it was.

"It's something beginning with *B*," Mia said, scratching her furry head.

The little Moss Mouse looked at the trees and plants that were growing all around her. Then she started to smile. "There must be lots of things in Misty Wood that begin with *B*," she said to herself. "If I keep looking for them, I'm

bound to remember what it was
that Mom wanted."

She swirled her wings and
whizzed off. Before long, she saw
a fluffy brown fairy animal with
floppy ears and beautiful golden
wings hopping along the ground.

"A Bud Bunny!" Mia cried.
"That begins with a *B*!"

She watched the bunny leaping
over ferns. Why would her mom
want a Bud Bunny? It looked much

too bouncy for the inside of Mia's burrow. And there weren't any buds there for it to open into flowers, which was the Bud Bunnies' special job.

"It can't be a Bud Bunny," Mia said, shaking her head.

34

Then she saw a big beech tree with wide branches stretching out like huge arms.

"Oooh—I know!" Mia cried, clapping her little paws together. "A beechwood back scratcher! Mom always has an itchy back."

But then Mia remembered that her dad had made her mom a beautiful back scratcher from a piece of beechwood only the other day.

35

"I don't think Mom would want *another* back scratcher," Mia said. "After all, she's only got one back!"

She flew on through the woods until she saw some water glinting in the sunlight.

"A babbling brook!" Mia squeaked. "Mom would love one of those!"

She glided down and landed softly on the bank of the brook. The water was fresh and clear and

36

made a cheerful gurgling noise as it rushed along.

Mia scampered across the bank. She sat down and leaned over to catch some of the water in her paws.

"Zzzz!"

Mia jumped and nearly tumbled into the brook. Something was buzzing around her head!

"Beeeeee careful," a buzzy voice said to her. "You don't want

to fall in." Then it stopped buzzing and landed on the bank in front of Mia. It was a fat, stripy bumblebee!

"Whatever are you doing?" the bee asked.

"I'm trying to catch the water," Mia told him. "My mom wants me to bring her a babbling brook."

"Well, that'zzz very strange," said the bumblebee. "Thizzz brook flowzzz on for milezzz and milezzz. It'zzz much too big to carry home."

Mia sighed. "Maybe I've got it wrong. All I know for sure is that she wants me to get her something beginning with *B*."

The bumblebee frowned.

"Your mom muzzzt have meant zzzomething elzzze," he buzzed.

Mia looked at him, and her whiskers started to tremble with excitement. "I know! Maybe Mom asked me to bring her a bumblebee!"

"Oh, I don't think so," the bee buzzed, backing away from Mia.

"We've got a lovely burrow," Mia said. "You'd really like it."

"But I need to be outzide, making lotzz of lovely honey from

40

flower nectar," he replied with a frown.

"Oh yes." Mia's whiskers began to droop. "Sorry, I didn't mean to upset you. It's probably not a bumblebee Mom wants after all. I just wish I could remember what it was."

She sat down on the grass and sniffed. She was feeling very fed up indeed. Her mom would be angry if she didn't remember!

The bumblebee rubbed his face with his front legs. "Don't be sad," he said. "What'z your name?"

Mia looked up at him. "Mia," she said quietly.

"I'm Buzby," he said. "Buzby the bumblebee. Look, Mia, there are loadzz of thingzz in Misty Wood beginning with *B*. I could help you look for them."

"Oh, thank you, Buzby!" Mia fluttered into the air.

42

"And just in case it *iz* a bumblebee she'z after," Buzby went on, "I'll come back with you to your burrow when we've finished looking. But only for a vizit. How about that?"

"That's so kind of you, Buzby," Mia said. She flapped her tiny wings happily. "Let's go!"

CHAPTER THREE

Searching Misty Wood!

Mia and Buzby fluttered through
the Heart of Misty Wood looking
for things beginning with *B*. All
around them, sunbeams poked

through the leaves like long golden fingers, making pretty patterns on the ground.

"Hey, Buzby!" Mia called. "There's a birch tree. That begins with a *B*."

The bumblebee zoomed over to the tall birch tree that Mia was pointing to. Beautiful pictures of hearts and rainbows had been carved into its silver bark by the Bark Badgers.

"Too big," Buzby buzzed. "It'll never fit inside your burrow."

But Mia's whiskers were twitching. "What about the twigs? We could make a bristly broomstick

46

with them! Maybe that's what
Mom wants."

Buzby looked doubtful. "Doezn't
she have one already?" he asked.

Mia nodded. "Yes, she does.
She sweeps the burrow with it every
day."

"Then she won't need another
one, will she? We'll have to look for
something elze."

They fluttered their wings
and flew on until they came to a

sunny clearing. A herd of Dream
Deer were bounding across the
grass. Their legs were so long
and they moved so gracefully
that they looked as if they were
dancing. Mia's whiskers twitched
and twizzled. Her next idea was so
much fun!

"Maybe Mom wants a ballet-
dancing buffalo!" she squeaked.
She was so excited she turned head
over heels in the air.

Buzby looked very surprised. "A buffalo? In Misty Wood? I've never seen one. Have you?"

"No, I suppose not," Mia said, spinning the right way up again.

"Your imagination'z running away with you," said Buzby. "Let'z head back. Keep looking for thingz beginning with *B*!"

Mia followed him through the trees. Buzby was a very serious bumblebee. Maybe she could think

of a story that would make him laugh. Her whiskers twizzled like mad.

"How about a boggley boogaloo!" she squeaked.

Buzby stared at Mia. "You just made that up, didn't you?" he buzzed.

"Yes, I did!" Mia giggled. Her whiskers twitched as more ideas popped into her head. "A boogaloo's a bright yellow bug, with big boggley eyes. And he

loves to . . . he loves to boogie! I could tell you a story about him if you like. . . ."

But Buzby wasn't listening. He'd seen something up ahead and he was zooming toward it, dodging between the tree trunks.

"Mia!" he called. "Come and zee!"

Mia's wings sparkled as she hurried after him.

"What did you find?"

52

"Down there," buzzed Buzby.

Mia looked down and saw a bramble bush stretching its thorny arms around the trunk of a tree. In between the thorns she could see . . .

"Blackberries!" she cried.

The two of them landed next to the bush. Sure enough, there were lots of juicy blackberries growing there, as shiny and bright as jewels.

"Are these what your mom wanted?" asked Buzby.

Mia scratched her head with her tiny pink paw. "I'm not sure," she said. "They do look delicious, though. Why don't we take some back to the burrow, just in case.

But there are so many—how will we carry them?"

Buzby twirled his antennae. "We need a bazket."

Mia's whiskers twitched. "Oh, Buzby—*basket* begins with *B*, too! Do you think that's what Mom wants?"

"I don't know," said Buzby. "But I know just where we can find one. Come on!"

He spun his little wings and

leaped into the air, flying swiftly toward the edge of Misty Wood. Mia followed him, and soon the trees began to thin out and she saw a long, leafy hedgerow.

There wasn't a basket to be seen. In fact, there wasn't anything at all beginning with *B*!

"Why did we come out here, Buzby?" she called out.

"Follow me," he buzzed, "and you'll see!"

CHAPTER FOUR

Follow the Song!

"Come on," Buzby called, pointing with his front legs as he flew up to the top of the hedge.

Mia raced after him. "Wow!" she gasped.

Hundreds of tiny, glittering dewdrops dangled from spiderwebs on the other side of the hedge. They looked like strings of diamonds.

"Those dewdrops are beautiful!" Mia cried. "What a shame they don't begin with *B*. Mom would love them!"

A white kitten with pale blue wings flew up to Mia. She was carrying a little basket made from woven flower stems.

58

Mia's whiskers began to twirl. "You're a Cobweb Kitten, aren't you?" she said.

The kitten nodded.

"It's your job to decorate the spiderwebs," Mia went on.

"That's right," purred the kitten.

59

"You've done such a lovely job!" Mia said.

"Thank you." The kitten smiled. "Do help yourself to some of my dewdrops."

"It's a bazket we need," Buzby interrupted. "We're looking for thingz beginning with *B*."

Mia nodded. "My mom asked me to bring her something beginning with *B*, and I've forgotten what it is," she explained

to the kitten. "We've found some lovely blackberries, but there are too many for us to carry. If we had a basket to put the blackberries in, we'd have two things beginning with *B*!"

"You can have my basket if you like," the friendly kitten said. "It's very light, and I've got loads more at home. I'll just hang these last few dewdrops."

Mia watched as the kitten flew

up and strung the bright droplets on the spider silk.

"Blackberries—how delicious," the kitten purred as she handed the empty basket to Mia. "I bet your mom will love them."

"I think so, too," Mia said. "I just hope they're what she asked me for. Thank you for your help!"

"Good luck," called the kitten as Mia and Buzby headed back to the blackberry bush.

"I hope we *will* be lucky," said Mia when they got back to the bush and began filling the basket.

"Shhh!" whispered Buzby. "Lizzen!"

High above their heads, a bird was singing.

"Twee-twee! Twee-twee-twee!"

Mia looked up. A little bird with bright blue feathers the color of a summer sky was circling high above them.

63

"A bluebird!"
Mia cried. "Maybe
that's what Mom
wanted. Quick, we've
got to catch up with him!"

Gripping the basket tightly in

her paws, Mia flew as fast as she could. But the little bird was too quick. His blue feathers flashed through the treetops as he darted away, singing, "Twee-twee! Twee-twee-twee!"

"Follow the song!" cried Mia.

"Phew!" panted Buzby, spinning his wings so fast they disappeared in a blur. "We'll never catch up with him!"

Suddenly, Buzby slowed down

and sniffed the air. "Ooh, Mia—what'z that lovely smell?"

A beautiful blue carpet of flowers stretched out on the ground below them. Mia and Buzby were flying over Bluebell Glade. But Mia didn't have time to think about

lovely smells. She just wanted to catch up with the bluebird.

"Come on, Buzby! Don't slow down!" she called.

"I've never seen so many flowerz before," panted Buzby.

"Twee-twee!" sang the bluebird,

far ahead of them. His voice was
getting fainter.

"Quick!" cried Mia. "We're
going to lose him!"

"I wish we could go and pick
some," Buzby sighed, looking down
at Bluebell Glade. "They smell so
nice."

"Buzby, forget the flowers!"
Mia cried. "Come on!"

But, try as they might, Mia
and Buzby couldn't keep up with

the bluebird. They whizzed along until they came to Heather Hill. The bluebird had disappeared. They couldn't even hear his song anymore.

"Do you think we could stop for a minute?" puffed Buzby. "I'm not used to flying so fast."

They flopped down on a patch of grass in among the heather. Lots of little yellow flowers were growing there, but Mia didn't notice them.

She felt really sad. She was quite sure that her mom had asked her for a bluebird, and now they had lost him.

Mia tried to cheer herself up by thinking about her story for Grandma. Maybe in the next part of the story, Archie the Ant could come to Heather Hill to search for his friend Clarissa. Maybe he'd look for her through the dark, shadowy places beneath the heather.

Mia peered between the twisty roots, imagining the little ant scurrying back and forth. There was no sign of Clarissa, but Mia noticed something else. Something blue.

"Buzby, what's that?" she said, pointing her paw at it.

"I'm not sure," Buzby replied. "I'll see if I can get it."

Buzby flattened his wings and squeezed between the heather plants. He came back holding a

beautiful bright blue feather in his antennae.

"It must have fallen when the bluebird flew over the hill," he said.

"It's so soft." Mia stroked the feather with her paw. "Maybe Mom wanted a bluebird's *feather*," she said, placing it in the basket. "But we'd better keep on looking for other things that begin with *B*."

"I begin with *B*!" a voice called out.

Mia was so surprised, she dropped the basket on her paw. "Who said that?" she squeaked as she rubbed her toe.

But there was no one there, just the little yellow flowers growing in the grass. Mia stared at them. They were buttercups. And *buttercups* began with *B*! It must have been a buttercup that spoke to her.

Mia picked some of the flowers and put them in the basket on top of the blackberries and the bluebird's feather.

"No!" came the voice again. "Not them, *me*!"

The voice was calling from up above. Whoever it was sounded very mad.

"Who's that?" Mia squeaked in her bravest voice, and she half covered her head with the basket.

CHAPTER FIVE

Seeing Stars

"Please don't hide," said the voice.

Mia peeped out from under

the little basket. An insect with big

purple wings was floating in the

76

air, gazing down at her with huge

eyes.

It was a beautiful butterfly.

"Hello!" the butterfly said,

swishing her wings. "I only shouted

77

at you because I was so excited. You see, I didn't always begin with *B*. In fact, up until last week, I began with *C*."

Mia and Buzby stared at the butterfly, puzzled.

"What do you mean?" Mia asked.

"Well, I used to be a caterpillar. But *now* I'm a beautiful, brilliant, brightly colored butterfly—so I most definitely begin with *B*!"

Mia's heart gave a big jump inside her. "Your name isn't Clarissa, is it?" she asked.

The butterfly looked surprised. "No. It's Buffy. Why do you ask?"

"Oh, never mind. It's just something to do with a story," Mia said. "It's very nice to meet you, Buffy. My name's Mia, and this is my friend Buzby."

"Nice to meet you, too," said Buffy.

Mia put her basket down and began to explain how her mom had asked her for something beginning with *B*. "I just can't remember what it was, though," she finished with a sigh.

"It might be blackberriez," Buzby said. "Or buttercupz. Or possibly a bumblebee like me. Or perhapz a bazket, or a bluebird'z feather, or—"

"A butterfly!" Mia interrupted,

her whiskers wiggling with
excitement.

"Really?" Buffy looked
pleased. "Well, of course, I *am* one
of the most beautiful butterflies in
Misty Wood, so I wouldn't be at
all surprised if it *is* me your mom
wants. Why don't I come along
with you?"

"Oh yes, would you?" Mia
cried. "I know my mom would love
your gorgeous wings."

81

"You could help us look for other thingz beginning with *B*, too," Buzby said, and he got up from the grass and stretched out his little legs. "Come on, let'z head back into Misty Wood!"

Buzby and Mia flew up to join Buffy as she fluttered off toward the trees. But Mia was so busy admiring Buffy's dazzling purple wings that she didn't look where she was going. All of a sudden—

82

oomph!—she flew straight into a big tree trunk. "Ouch!" squeaked Mia as she slid down the trunk and landed with a thud.

"Oh no! Did you hurt yourself?" asked Buzby, landing softly on the ground beside her.

"Oooh," said Mia, "what lovely twinkly stars . . . pink ones and silver ones and—"

"Starz?" said Buzby, looking around. "Where?"

"She's seeing stars because she bumped her head," Buffy explained, fanning Mia with her wings. "Are you okay?"

"Yes, I think so," Mia said,

sitting up carefully. The stars had all disappeared now. "It wasn't a bad bump. Thanks, Buffy."

Something had fallen off the tree as Mia slid down it. She picked it up. It was a piece of bark.

"Maybe it was some bark Mom wanted!" she said.

She turned the bark over and saw that it was covered in swirly lines and circles.

"What a beautiful pattern.

A Bark Badger must have made it,"
Buffy said.

"Hey!" a gruff voice called.

Mia jumped in surprise. A
stocky Bark Badger with a black-
and-white-striped face and shiny
silver wings was coming toward
them. It must have been his tree
she'd bumped into! "I'm so s-s-
sorry!" she stammered. "I didn't
mean to knock your bark off the
tree. It was an accident, I promise."

The badger threw back his head and gave a loud, hearty laugh.

"Don't worry, little Moss Mouse," he said in a booming voice. "You can keep that piece if you like."

Mia heaved a sigh of relief. "Thanks!" she said. "My friends and I are collecting as many things beginning with *B* as we can find— for my mom."

"I see." The Bark Badger nodded kindly. "Can I help?" he asked.

"Wait a minute!" Buffy's purple wings started to quiver. "It might be a *Bark Badger* that your mom wants, Mia."

Mia looked at the badger's big shoulders and his rough gray fur. It would be a tight squeeze fitting him into the burrow—but maybe Buffy was right.

"It *could* be a Bark Badger," she said. "But I'm not sure. Oh, I wish I could remember!"

The badger smiled. "Well, why don't I come with you?" he said. "Just in case it *is* a Bark Badger you need. My name's Barney, by the way."

"Thank you so much!" Mia cried. "Look at everything we've collected!"

She held up her little pink paws and began counting on her fingers.

"A bumblebee, a butterfly, a Bark Badger, a bluebird's feather,

90

a piece of bark, and a basket full
of buttercups and blackberries!"
She looked at her new friends
and smiled. "I think we must have
everything beginning with *B* in the
whole of Misty Wood. Thank you,
everyone!"

The others smiled.

Buzby looked up at the sky.
"The sun'z going down," he said.
"Iz it teatime yet?"

"It must be," said Mia. "Come

on, let's head back to the burrow.
I bet Mom's made a cake."

Barney picked up the basket,
and the four friends flew off
through Misty Wood, with Mia
leading the way.

CHAPTER SIX

Two Happy Endings

Mia scampered down the tunnel that led to her burrow, her new friends close behind her. "Come meet my mom, everyone!" she called.

Mia's mom looked up in surprise as first Mia, then Buzby, then Buffy, and finally Barney squeezed into the burrow.

"Well, I'm very glad I made such a big cake for tea," she said. "Mia, did you remember to bring—"

But Mia didn't let her mom finish. "I've brought lots of things!" she squeaked excitedly. "Let's go over to Grandma's bed, and I'll show them to you!"

Mia's mom looked puzzled.

Mia scampered over, with Buzby flying along at her side.

"I do hope we got the thing my mom wanted," she whispered to him.

"I'm sure you did," Buzby hummed, close to her ear. "We have so many thingz beginning with *B*."

Grandma's little black eyes nearly popped out of her head when she saw all the visitors.

"Well, well, well!" she said. "This is a surprise! Pull up a cushion, why don't you? There's plenty of them."

Barney the Bark Badger grinned as he sat down. He was much too big to stand up in the burrow. He kept bumping his wings on the ceiling.

Mia looked at her mom. "I know you wanted something beginning with *B*," she started

TWO HAPPY ENDINGS

to explain, "but I forgot what it was. So I brought you everything beginning with *B* that I could find. There's a bumblebee. . . ."

Buzby stood up and gave a little bow. "Buzby, at your service, ma'am," he said.

"Lovely to meet you, Buzby," Mia's mom said. "But I'm afraid it wasn't a bumblebee I wanted."

"Well, how about a butterfly?" asked Mia. "This is Buffy."

Buffy gave a twirl so that everyone could see her pretty lilac wings.

Mia's mom shook her head. "You look lovely, Buffy. But it wasn't a butterfly I was after."

"Oh, dear." Mia was beginning to feel worried. "Was it a Bark Badger, Mom? Because I brought Barney just in case."

Barney raised a front paw. "How do you do?" he said

grandly. "I'm very happy to help out however I can."

"That's very good of you," Mia's mom said. "But I'm afraid I don't need a Bark Badger, either."

Mia bit her lip. This wasn't going well at all. She picked up the basket.

"How about this lovely basket?"

Mia's mom shook her head.

Mia's whiskers drooped down below her mouth.

"Show her what'z inside the bazket!" Buzby buzzed quietly. "There are still lotz of thingz beginning with *B*."

"Okay," Mia whispered. She pulled out the bluebird's feather and showed it to her mom. "Was it this?"

"No, Mia," her mom replied. "But that's a nice feather. I can weave it into the quilt I'm making for the babies' cot."

101

"What about this?" Mia held up the piece of bark.

"Bark's always useful," Mia's mom said. "And I love the pattern. But I didn't ask for a piece of bark. What I wanted was—"

"These?" Mia squeaked, tipping up the basket so that all the juicy blackberries spilled out.

"No, not blackberries, though they'll be lovely to have with our tea," Mia's mom said.

There was just one thing left.

"Buttercups!" cried Mia, holding up the bunch of bright yellow flowers. "Please tell me you wanted buttercups!"

Mia's mom sighed. "No, Mia. I'm sorry, but it wasn't buttercups I asked you to bring, either."

Mia sat back on her hind legs and sighed. "What in Misty Wood could it be? I thought I'd collected *everything* beginning with *B*."

"Bluebells," Mia's mom said gently. "I asked for some bluebells."

"Some *bluebells*?" Mia gasped.

"Oh no!" groaned Buzby. He hid his face in his front legs. "Mia—

we flew over hundredz of them
in Bluebell Glade . . ."

Mia nodded. "Yes, when we
were chasing the bluebird. We didn't
stop to think. What do you want the
bluebells for, Mom?"

"To put on the cushion you
made for Grandma," Mia's mom
said. "All it needs are some bluebell
decorations to make it quite perfect."

"Grandma, I'm so sorry!" Mia
burst into tears. "I've been a silly

Moss Mouse. Your cushion would have looked so pretty with some bluebells to finish it off!"

Grandma's nose wrinkled in a smile.

"Don't cry, Mia," she said. "I'm not upset that you forgot about the bluebells. Because you *did* bring some buttercups—and they're my favorite flowers in the world!"

"Really?" Mia sniffed.

"Really and truly," her

grandma replied. "They're so very bright and cheerful, they make me think of sunshine. I'd much rather have buttercups than bluebells on my cushion."

Mia wiped her eyes and fixed some of the buttercups onto Grandma's moss cushion. They looked beautiful, and everybody clapped and cheered.

"Well done," said Mia's mom. "You might have forgotten the

bluebells, Mia, but you've made Grandma very happy with those buttercups. Now, shall I get the tea?"

Buzby, Buffy, and Barney all said they would help.

"I'll come, too!" Mia said.

Grandma shook her head. "Stay here with me, Mia," she said. "I want to hear the rest of your story. Sit on the buttercup cushion beside me and tell me more about Clarissa the Caterpillar."

Mia jumped onto the cushion. "D'you remember, Grandma, how Clarissa disappeared, and her friend Archie the Ant couldn't find her?" she asked.

Grandma nodded.

"Well . . ." Mia's whiskers wiggled. She told Grandma how Archie had searched everywhere. He'd climbed up a big tall tree— how scary that was! And he'd hunted all through the roots of the

heather plants on Heather Hill, but Clarissa was nowhere to be seen.

"So where was she?" Grandma asked.

Mia's whiskers were twizzling so much. She knew Grandma would love the end of the story.

"There was one place Archie hadn't looked—Moonshine Pond. He trudged all the way there through Misty Wood. His legs were aching so much he could hardly walk."

"Poor Archie," said Grandma. "I feel quite sorry for him."

"When he got to the pond, there was no sign of Clarissa," Mia went on. "There was only a beautiful butterfly admiring her reflection in the water. Archie started to cry. 'I miss my friend Clarissa!' he said. The butterfly flew over and sat beside him on the grass. 'Don't be sad,' she said. 'It's me. *I'm* Clarissa.'"

"Well, I never!" Grandma said.

"Archie didn't believe her," continued Mia. "But Clarissa explained that all caterpillars eat lots and lots and get bigger and bigger, and then they disappear for a while until they turn into butterflies. She thanked Archie for bringing her all those lovely snacks to eat when she had been a caterpillar.

"'You've helped me become the

most beautiful butterfly in Misty Wood,' she said. 'I'll be your best friend for ever and ever.' Archie was so happy he forgot how tired he was and danced all the way around Moonshine Pond. The end!"

"Oh, Mia!" said Grandma with a big smile. "I love a happy ending."

"Did I hear someone say 'snacks'?" called Mia's mom. She trotted up to Grandma's bed,

carrying the piece of bark. On top of it was a cake made from crunchy hazelnuts.

Buzby and Buffy followed her, carrying acorns filled with blackberry juice. Mia's dad came over, too, with some plump barleycorns he'd found while he was out collecting moss.

And last of all came Barney, who was carrying Mia's baby brothers and sisters in the basket

so that they could join in the tea party.

Everybody sat down around Grandma and began eating and drinking. Mia snuggled up with Grandma in her mossy bed, and nibbled some cake.

"Look at all the things I found!" she said when she had finished her cake. "A bumblebee, blackberries, a basket, and a butterfly . . ."

"I can think of something else beginning with *B*," Grandma whispered when Mia got to the end of the list.

"What?" asked Mia, looking around. She saw the grains of barley that her dad had brought.

"Is it *barleycorns*, Grandma?"

"They're tasty, but no, that's not what I meant," Grandma said.

Then Mia saw her four brothers and sisters sipping their blackberry

117

juice. "Do you mean *babies*, Grandma?"

Grandma laughed. "That's a good guess! But no. You've brought so many wonderful things today, Mia—especially those beautiful buttercups. But the most special thing of all is that I feel *better*. You told me such a lovely story and made me such a beautiful cushion that I forgot all about my cold. It's quite gone away! You've made me

118

feel *better*, and that's the *best* thing of all."

Mia looked at Grandma's smiling face. Then she looked at her mom, who was showing Buzby and Buffy and Barney how to make a moss cushion. They weren't very good at it, and everybody was laughing and giggling as they rolled the moss around. Then she looked at her dad, who was tickling the babies

with the bluebird's feather and

making them laugh.

Everybody was so happy.

Perhaps I'm not so silly after all, Mia thought, and she cuddled up next to Grandma and helped herself to another piece of her mom's delicious cake.

Turn the page for
lots of fun
Misty Wood
activities!

Mia's mom asked her
to find some **bluebells**.
Can you help Mia follow
the right path?

Mia spent the day in Misty Wood trying to find things beginning with *B*. She found lots and lots of things!

Why not go on a treasure hunt in your garden, or in the park with your parent or guardian?

Write down all the things you find.

Things beginning with A

_____

_____

_____

Things beginning with B

_____

_____

_____

Things beginning with C

_____

_____

_____

Spot the Difference

The picture on the opposite page is slightly different from this one. Can you circle all the differences?

Moss Mice, like Mia, love making and decorating soft, beautiful moss cushions for the fairy animals to sleep on.

Use the outline on the next page to design and decorate your very own moss cushion!

Misty Wood Word Search

Use the words below to create your own word search! Write all the words in the boxes, then fill the other spaces with lots of different letters.
See if a friend can solve it!

BADGER
BARK
BLUEBELLS
BUZBY
CUSHION
MOSS
PAWS
STORY
WINGS

Fairy Animals

of Misty Wood

Meet more **Fairy Animal** friends!

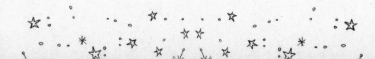